AF578528

ENVELOPE

IQ MISKAL

ENVELOPE

© COPYRIGHT 2022 IQ MISKAL - ALL RIGHTS RESERVED.

The content contained within this book may not be reproduced, duplicated or transmitted without direct written permission from the author or the publisher.

Under no circumstances will any blame or legal responsibility be held against the publisher, or author, for any damages, reparation, or monetary loss due to the information contained within this book. Either directly or indirectly.

Legal Notice:

This book is copyright protected. This book is only for personal use. You cannot amend, distribute, sell, use, quote or paraphrase any part, or the content within this book, without the consent of the author or publisher.

Disclaimer Notice:

Please note the information contained within this document is for educational and entertainment purposes only. All effort has been executed to present accurate, up to date, and reliable, complete information. No warranties of any kind are declared or implied. Readers acknowledge that the author is not engaging in the rendering of legal, financial, medical or professional advice. The content within this book has been derived from various sources. Please consult a licensed professional before attempting any techniques outlined in this book.

By reading this document, the reader agrees that under no circumstances is the author responsible for any losses, direct or indirect, which are incurred as a result of the use of the information contained within this document, including, but not limited to, — errors, omissions, or inaccuracies.

TABLE OF CONTENTS

PART 1

Naturally, I was stunned to see my dead wife walking down the street with a young man. Is it possible for a deceased person to walk down the street in such a graceful manner? But I buried Nishi with my own hands. And besides, Nishi doesn't have a twin sister to walk like this behind my eyes.

Thinking about this, when I looked at that place again, I did not see a woman who was like my wife. Because of my stupidity, I now want to kill myself. Still, with some hope in my heart, I reached where the girl was standing with a young man.

This intersection of New York is so full of localities that it will not take time for anyone to lose sight of the target in the blink of an eye. After arriving at the place and looking around, I saw the girl again when I was giving up hope. But by the time I crossed the road to reach the area, the girl had boarded a bus, and the bus immediately left. When a heavy vehicle hit me, I was about to get on my bike in the opposite direction to follow the girl out of curiosity. Due to a severe head injury, I became unconscious for a moment, and then I didn't remember anything else.

When I opened my eyes, I found myself in a hospital bed. I turned around and saw my current wife, Mimi, eagerly waiting for me to regain consciousness. After a while, my brother-in-law Mihad entered our cabin with a nurse. The nurse put her hand on my forehead and checked my pulse to determine my body. At that moment, my wife Mimi said to me,

- What happened to you? How did the accident happen? Tell me.

Along with Mimi, my brother-in-law Mihad also said,

- Brother! Hearing the news of your accident, my sister went crazy. How did the accident happen? Tell us.

I didn't say anything after seeing these dramas of Mimi and Mihad. Because I have spent these few days watching them.

After coming home after being released from the hospital, I kept thinking about that girl who looked exactly like Nishi. Seeing me drowning in the world of thoughts, Mimi made soup for me at night and asked,

- Well, you don't talk to me well, so you can't share the news of the accident with me today?

- Today, I saw a girl like Nishi on the street. I did not understand what happened when I went to the girl.

Mimi was quite startled by my words.

- What do you say? How would Nishi come back to the streets when she was dead? Maybe that was a mistake in your mind. Well, now put those thoughts aside, and I have something to say.

-Hmm, you need money.

Mimi said somewhat hesitantly at my words.

- Yes, father will cultivate some vegetables in the land, so he told me that you should give him $10k. No problem, he will pay you again after selling the vegetables.

Without replying to Mimi's words, I left the room and went to the roof. I know that since Mimi's father asked for money, I have to pay him against my will, and that is only because of my mother.

I got married to Mimi last month. Before Mimi, I was married to a girl named Nishi. But within a year of marriage, Nishi mysteriously committed suicide.

The incident was a year ago...

I had just been promoted to the Ministry from Field Officer of the Department of Transportation. I loved Nishi very much because she was perfect for me as a wife. And besides, her relationship with me was also amicable. One day I had to go from New York to California due to an urgent need for office work. That day I left Nishi alone at home, and even then, Nishi was usually alone. Sometimes our maid used to do some minor work. One day after reaching California, I suddenly got a maid's call and immediately left for New York again. When I saw Nishi's hanging body when I arrived home, my heart turned into a pitch black darkness. I still could not think why Nishi committed suicide. Just then, an officer in charge of the police took me aside during interrogation and told me that our gate security guard had done something terrible to Nishi, so she could not accept the loss of her honour and committed suicide. And all this was mentioned in the letter kept on Nishi's table. They even said that the security guard was still engaged in the security work of the house, so we caught him quickly. The rest will be known in the postmortem report. Even if he doesn't tell the truth now, he will tell everything if he is taken inside the prison and beaten.

At that time, I did not listen to the words of the police because the security guard could never do bad things to my wife with such courage. Moreover, the security guard was supposed to run away immediately after this incident, but he was still in the house. However, Nishi told me one day that the security guard would often look at her with evil eyes when she was leaving the house.

These strange thoughts arose in my mind that day, but later the post-mortem report and the security guard's confession proved all my earlier thoughts false.

This painful death of Nishi made my life miserable. But mysteriously, a parcel arrived in my name about a month after Nishi's death. When I opened the package, I was transfixed for a limited time by the paper inside. Because there was a divorce paper inside it and Nishi's signature on it, it can't be a normal thing to get a divorce paper from my wife a month after her death. After that, although I tried many times to unravel the mystery of all this, I did not get any results from that mystery.

Standing on the roof and thinking about those sad moments of the past, I brought the watch in front my eyes. I don't know when the two hours passed. I was not hurt so much in today's accident, but my hand and head were severely injured. As it was quite a night, I knocked on the house door from the roof.

After knocking, Mimi opened the door. Honestly, I can't stand this girl at all. Mimi is my cousin. My mother first wanted to marry me to Mimi. But seeing that my father and I disagreed on this matter, she could not proceed any further. Mimi was inferior in quality, but all her family members were greedy. Mimi's father played many tricks with me to get Mimi married at first, but nothing worked. Although after Nishi's death, their wish was fulfilled a little late. Mimi girl is not as bad as her family, but I can't stand her at all because of her family's low mentality. Within a month of the wedding, Mimi's father has already taken $2k from me through Mimi. However, my mother is behind it. Because she is so stupid that she can't get rid of her delusion even if someone fools her.

When I expressed my reluctance to loan, my mother said,

- If one of the relatives is poor, we should be helped with money. And Mimi's father is our relative from both sides. He said he would take your money and give it back, so why do you do that?

I was forced to loan money because of my mother's statement, and I know well that I will never get this money back alive. Besides, my brother-in-law Mihad also studies from here and I have to bear his entire expenses. Considering all this, I am distraught with Mimi because if I had not married her, Mimi's father would never have had the opportunity to ask me for money so quickly, and I would not have given him more than once.

However, the next day when I was busy with office work, I suddenly received a call from an unknown number. While in the office, I do not receive numbers known, and there is no question of receiving unknown numbers. So after calling again, I kept the mobile silent instead of not receiving it.

When I was eating at night, I thought of that unknown number. Out of curiosity, I called that number after finishing my meal. A young man from the other side said to receive,

-Sir, a parcel has arrived for you by courier.

I asked pretty surprised.

- There was no talk of anyone giving me a parcel.

- You may not remember, and we will take the parcel from our branch tomorrow.

I hung up the call without saying anything else and thinking,

- Why will someone give me a parcel without saying anything?

However, after ending my thoughts, when I arrived at the courier office the next day, a boy in charge matched my number and handed me a letter-like parcel. I still didn't know what was inside, so I couldn't contain my curiosity and tore open the letter and took out the paper inside. But seeing a sentence written in big letters on the article, a strange shiver ran through my body instantly. I mean that what I thought in this one year was right?

PART 2

But even then, I could not think who had sent me this parcel and what the purpose of sending this sentence is.

Today, I could not concentrate properly in the office due to this parcel mystery. Because I did not think I would face two secrets two days in a row. But one thing I can't reconcile in any way is the girl I saw on the street that day that looked precisely like Nishi, was she Nishi's twin sister or someone else? As I heard somewhere that there could be seven people with the same face in the world, it is never believable for me to have such a resemblance.

After returning home at night, I carefully turned over the paper in the parcel, but nothing else was written on that paper except the sentence printed in bold letters. Suddenly I thought that when a packet arrived from the courier, they would also give me the slip with the sender's name and mobile number. But how stupid I was, I forgot to take the slip in my eagerness for the parcel. Still, I breathed a little sigh of relief, thinking that tomorrow, with the slip from the courier office, it would be understood who was playing with me by giving such a parcel.

Thinking this, I carefully put the paper in the letter inside my personal office bag. Immediately Mimi entered the room and said to me,

- Well, did you think about your father's money? Dad said it's a little better if you give the money tomorrow! I will buy vegetable seeds tomorrow.

I had been a silent listener to Mimi's words for a long time, but today, my patience broke due to some unknown reason. I said in a furious voice,

-Listen! Your father does not get any money from me; I will give him money only when he needs it. Girls like you come to the son-in-law's house to empty the son-in-law's pocket and to make the father rich. That's why I didn't agree to marry you the first time. Are you not ashamed to ask me for money for your father? Girls bring more from your father's house, and you do the opposite. And I know very well that no matter how much money I give to your father, I will not be lucky enough to get a single penny back from him. I thought you were not as greedy as your father, but you proved me wrong after marriage.

Mimi could not digest my words and naturally let out tears in her eyes. But why did these expressions of hers look so ugly to me? Soon after, Mimi left the bedroom, and I slowly moved the body on the bed without paying attention to her.

When I woke up, I saw my brother-in-law, Mihad, packing the luggage. I asked him in a curious tone.

- Where do you go?

Mihad said somewhat hesitantly.

-Sister says if I am here, she has to face many problems. So she told me to stay in a separate house.

I was pretty shocked after hearing Mihad's words, and after that, I got a little angry in my mind and went to the balcony to see Mimi talking to someone on the phone angrily. At the moment of speaking, I stood in front of the balcony door without disturbing her and tried to listen to her words. As far as I understand, Mimi is talking to her father, and as a result of repeatedly asking me for money through her, she is telling her father,

-If you don't want to see me happy, you don't need to talk to me anymore. Do you know how much humiliation I accept when asking for money? You have married me here for your own sake, not even thinking about your daughter's happiness in life. I say one thing very well today: if you ever ask my husband for money, you will never get your daughter again.

Saying this, Mimi hung up the phone and tried vainly to wipe the tears from her eyes. She didn't even notice that I was standing behind her, listening to their entire conversation. My resentment towards Mimi has been working for a long time, but today I feel sorry for myself that it was wrong to mistreat Mimi yesterday. Because here there is no fault of her, she is being used by making sesame oil. And besides, my father-in-law is like my father, so if he needs any help, as a son-in-law, I must help him. Thinking of this, she was a little surprised as I put my hand on Mimi's shoulder. Mimi was surprised to see my sudden presence, but she did not understand that I had heard her words. I asked her in a very calm tone, although she was angry a little earlier.

- Where did you ask Mihad to go?

At my words, she said in a very hesitant manner,

-No, what will he do from here? Since he has come to study, let him learn with a bit of difficulty. If he doesn't suffer, what will he know well?

- You can lie well. What is the lack of space here for him to study? And I prepared the money for my father-in-law. Tell him to come and take it away. I will go to the office now, give me food quickly, there is not much time.

Mimi is looking at me with surprised eyes hearing my words. She never expected such a message from me this time.

- Why are you looking like this?

-No means nothing. But please don't give the money to my father, because you rightly said it would not be returned if you provided the money to the father.

- You don't have to worry about that. I don't have a problem if I don't get the money back, my father-in-law is like my father, and I don't have a problem if he doesn't pay me back.

With this, I returned and came to the dining room with a little smile. I know Mimi can't see my smile but is watching me in amazement as I walk. On reaching the dining room, I said to Mihad in a very bright voice,

- Do you always have to listen to your stupid sister? Fools say so many things. Go to your room with everything.

Mihad's darkened face brightened instantly at my words.

Mimi has taken good care of me these few days since marriage, but today I don't know why I am getting a little more insight into everything. Although I had a good laugh about this in my heart, I did not express it.

As soon as I came to the office, I remembered yesterday's parcel again. My office colleague Nazrul and I are almost the same age, and my relationship with him is slightly different from others. Although I rarely talk to everyone, I share everything I have with Nazrul. And the main reason for this is that he is a very clever man who quickly solves any problem. I breathed a sigh of relief when I met him today as he was on leave for the last three days. As I walked to his desk, he hugged me like a long-lost friend. I like him a little bit more because of his innocent behaviour. Then I said to him after exchanging compliments.

- Nazrul brother, lately I have been stuck in many mysteries. I feel like someone is playing with me.

He said to me in a rather curious tone,

-What happened?

I told him about Nishi's similar girl and parcels one by one. He said with a slightly worried face.

- Hmm, that's something to think about. But seeing that girl may be a mistake of your eyes, but the matter of the parcel is extraordinary. Moreover, one year after the death of your wife, why would someone try to tell you the old story again? Well, the slip of the parcel should have the sender's number. Did you bring it?

- No, brother. For the parcel's curiosity, I did not remember to take it at all.

- You did a stupid thing. I will return to the courier office this afternoon and bring the slip. If you call that number, you can understand who it is.

After talking with Nazrul brother for a while, I was

about to go back to my desk when I got a call from an unknown number. I usually don't take calls during office hours, but today I received the call for some reason. As soon as I received it, a female voice told me from the other side,

-Sir, a parcel has arrived for you, and please take it from our branch.

As soon as I heard this, I ran to Nazrul Brother's desk and said,

- Brother, another parcel has arrived again.

- Give me the phone.

As I handed the phone to him, he said,

-Where did the parcel come from?

The girl on the other end could be heard very clearly as the call was put on loudspeaker. The girl replied to her words,

-Yes, sir, from the Colorado branch.

I was shocked to hear this.

- Nazrul brother, Colorado, was at my previous wife's father's house.

He was also quite surprised at my words and said,

-Let's go, today I will also go with you to bring the parcel.

I arrived at the courier office with Nazrul brother after the afternoon off with a lot of curiosity. Seeing that my number matched the number on the parcel, the boy in charge handed me a letter-like paper as before. Without a moment's delay, I said,

-A parcel arrived yesterday too, but I didn't remember to take the slip. Can that slip be given now?

-Yes, sir, of course.

That's why the boy handed me today's and yesterday's slip.

I was shocked to see my first wife Nishi's old number on both slips in the sender's place. How is this possible? I destroyed Nishi's SIM after her death. So how did her number come here again?

PART 3

Seeing the curious expression on my face, Nazrul brother asked,

- Is there a problem, brother?

At his words, I turned to him and said,

- Brother, here is my first wife's number, but I broke her SIM then.

He was also a little surprised by my words. He immediately said,

- Well, brother, call the number and see if the phone is ringing.

As he said, I took out the phone from my pocket and dialled the number. But I was very disappointed to hear the familiar message of the SIM Company, that is, the number is closed. Nazrul brother understood the matter and said,

-Brother, someone may be joking about confusing you. It will help if you put these thoughts out of your head for now. The more you delve into these nonsense mysteries, the more secrets will grow. Well,

I saw the paper.

I could not comfort my mind in any way with Nazrul brother's words, but as he said, he saw today's and yesterday's letters. As he turned the two letters over, he also carefully examined the paper on top of the letter.

- Brother, these were not sent from Colorado but someone from New York.

I was immediately surprised by his words and asked,

- How did you understand?

He held the paper above the letter before my eyes and said,

- See what is written on the paper? XYZ Food and Beverage Ltd., New York, USA. That means the inner paper is a standard printed paper, but the upper packet is not a formal paper. These packets are available in New York city. And different people make different types of open packets or letter packets from the waste paper of these companies. Now the question arises in your mind how did I know all this? Quite some time ago, I went to our local mosque to distribute sweets packets on Fridays and go local market to collect empty boxes. Usually, people give sweets in jute paper packets, but I couldn't find them then, so I was forced to provide sweets in this type of paper packet.

- Hmm, brother, I understand that it was sent from inside Dhaka, then why give the name of Colorado on the sender's place on the parcel?

- Hey brother, is the parcel provider as thick-headed as you? He is sending these strange parcels to confuse you. Why write the original name of the place?

- I understand that brother, but the name of the place where the parcel is sent is mentioned in the courier service, so what is the reason for it being an exception?

- Hmm, the brother said a wise thing. I'm looking into the matter.

With this, he again went forward in front of the boy who was in charge of the courier and said,

Brother, who is responsible for exchanging your parcels?

- Sorry, sir! You can tell us if there are any errors in your parcel. Sharing of personal information is prohibited here.

-Brother, you come to the side, and there was something to talk about.

As soon as the boy went to the side, as per Nazrul brother's words, he stuffed a shiny new $100 into the boy's pocket and said something. Soon the boy's dull face was full of smiles. After explaining something to the boy for some time, he immediately came in front of me, and I asked him with a somewhat curious look at his actions.

- What did you say, brother? And what did you pay for?

- It is the same as playing riddles with stupid people and feeding grass to goats. Brother, if you keep collecting the parcels like this, you will never find the real trickster. Remember that if someone takes a step forward to make you hesitate, you should take two steps forward instead of behind them.

I think since it has sent two parcels two days in a row, it will send again tomorrow. And tomorrow, the mystery will be revealed whether the parcels have come from far Colorado or someone from New York is having fun sending them.

But one thing I don't understand is why the reason is for your first wife's death repeatedly indicated in the parcel.

- Hmm, brother! That's why I can't sleep at night.

- Let's go home now without worrying so much. Tomorrow the game will start directly on the field.

After saying goodbye to Nazrul brother, I left for home. Even if he sometimes talks rudely about me, I don't feel bad because I can't understand even simple things. But he gets the details right with his subtle thinking, and that's why I like him the most.

When I came home, I saw that Mimi's father, my father-in-law, had come to collect money from me. Although I told Mimi yesterday that giving money to my father-in-law is the same as giving money to my father, to be honest, I did not say that from my heart.

Because the main reason I wouldn't say I like Mimi's father is not because of his repeated requests for money but because of their family's evil deeds. I heard from my father that Mimi's fathers were once big dacoits and ransacked the rich man in the countryside. But once their influence and prestige decreased, they returned to everyday life. But this stigma did not leave their way.

Since they were on a good path, the ordinary people took advantage of the opportunity, united them and drove them out of the village. At one point, he developed a love relationship with Mimi's mother, my aunt. But because of their tainted past, no family in the town would agree to give them a daughter; even my grandmother was no exception.

When they left the village, he got angry with Mimi's mother because she had no choice. Even though my grandfather disowned her daughter for such activities, my mother could not overcome her love for her beloved sister. As a result, he wanted to marry Mimi from the beginning to keep the sister around her.

Mimi's father was very busy in our house. My father never dared to ask for money as he did not like him. Since I got a government job after graduation, his visits to our house increased. But despite my mother's approval, she could not proceed because my father could see her primary purpose. He and his family did not come to my wedding when I married Nishi. But the most surprising thing is that after three months of marrying Nishi, even though he did not step foot in our house, he used to come to our home in such a cheerful and cheerful manner that I saw last after getting my government job.

So much for the past. As soon as I entered the house, Mimi's father approached me politely and asked,

- How are you, father?

I said with a little smile that I was fine, but I was telling the truth in my heart.

-That past habit of opportunistic people like you is not gone yet. What money will I give you so easily?

I returned to reality from these thoughts and looked at Mimi standing in front of the kitchen. I saw a lot of excitement on her face. No matter how nasty my father-in-law is, Mimi and my brother-in-law Mihad's mind is as simple as water. Mimi is happy with little things, and her tendency to have patience is very high. Even if I scold her, she will listen to everything like a silent listener but will not reply.

-Mimi! What did you cook for your father?

- Yes, I cooked beef and chicken for dad.

- Well.

And then I went to my bedroom. My main objective now is to turn Mimi's father around in various ways and test his endurance. If I give him $10k so quickly, he will get greedy and ask for money again.

Putting this thought aside, for now, I took up today's parcel letter. At that time, trying to solve the mystery of that number, I didn't even remember to look at the text inside the letter. So I put the letters in yesterday's and today's parcel side by side on the table and tried to find out the link between the two. In the first letter, in bold letters,

"Your wife did not commit suicide but was murdered."

And secondly, in today's letter, very clearly and boldly,

"The murderer may have been someone close to you."

After reading the second letter, I was pretty worried. Means someone around me? Who could it be? And who is giving this letter? As I was getting lost in the mystery of these things, I was startled by Mimi's call. Hiding the two letters, I asked in a slightly angry tone,

- What happened?

- No, I mean father's money...

-Actually, I forgot to withdraw the money from the bank today. I will give him tomorrow and ask him to stay at home today.

Mimi also said, quite happily.

- Well, I do.

The next day I was sitting in the office talking with Nazrul brother about the parcel, just then I got a call on my mobile from an unknown number. Nazrul brother said to me in a cheerful tone,

- Did you see that the parcel is still being talked about today?

As soon as he received the call, a young man from the other side said with the familiar words,

A parcel has arrived in your name, and please take it from our branch.

After listening to the parcel for the past two days, I did not feel anything, but today, the mercury of excitement in my body has risen to the top due to some unknown reason. Nazrul brother said with a mysterious smile.

- Didn't I say, brother, I will send the parcel again today? And it is not possible to send parcels from Colorado every day, and it is only possible to send from New York. Do you understand?

- Then we will bring the parcel to the office.

- Not only to bring the parcel but also to find out who is having fun with you today.

I am sometimes really surprised by Nazrul brother's forward thinking. If he had become a detective instead of doing this job, there would have been no mystery in any case.

I arrived at the courier office after the break with curiosity and excitement. After checking my number and picking up the parcel, I saw that the same falsified letter was sent to us two days ago, and today it is the same. Nazrul brother took me away and said something to the boy whom I had bribed yesterday. In the middle of talking with Nazrul brother, the boy called someone and brought him to us. The boy he called was not very old but was engaged in parcel exchange as far as I could tell. When I went to Nazrul brother, he asked the boy,

-Where did you get this parcel from?

- Where will I bring it again? Since Colorado is written here, I have brought it from Colorado.

- Don't lie. I know parcels don't arrive daily from Colorado; there is at least a two-day gap. But similar parcels have been coming to us for the last two days.

Nazrul brother's words made the boy quite stupid, but he could not accept it in any way. Nazrul Brother understood the matter and put a $100 in the boy's pocket and said,

-Now tell me, where did you get it from?

The boy took the money in his hands and said in a very hesitant manner,

- Yes, brother, but it is acceptable to say these things, but I am saying that it has been sent from the New York's other branch. These hide parcels cost a bit more to send as the location name, and mobile number differ.

- Hmm, I understand. I will give you another $100 if you go with us to that branch now.

After listening to him, the boy refused for a long time, but at one stage, after being persuaded by Nazrul brother's words, the boy agreed to go.

We are now standing at that courier branch. Nazrul brother called the one in charge there,

- Well, brother, we have received parcels three days in a row, but I don't know who is sending them. Can you see your CCTV footage?

- Sorry, sir! Showing footage to outsiders is not allowed.

Is it within your rules that you are harassing us by

sending such hide parcels?

At one point, when the man was arguing with Nazrul brother, he suddenly said,

- Do you know who I am? If you don't show me the footage, I will complain to the police now. Because of you, they are sending me these strange parcels and threatening to kill me.

I was surprised by Nazrul brother's words. Because the parcel is sending me, and then they threaten me to kill?

Soon after, the leading man in charge there got terrified and comforted Nazrul brother and said,

- Please calm down, and I will show you the footage. Come here.

Seeing their defeat, I understood that it was also a trick of Nazrul brother.

Then the man started showing us the recorded footage from the morning. Suddenly at a place, I asked them to stop. Nazrul brother was quite surprised and asked,

- What brother did you get?

-Yes, this girl looks familiar, but the camera is above her head, so the face is not visible.

Hearing my words, Nazrul brother said to the man,

-Any more footage to see this girl?

-Yes, brother.

This is why he turned on another footage. Then when he brought the footage in real-time, I reached the limit of surprise. It was the girl who resembled my first wife whom I first saw walking down the street with a young man. How is this possible?

PART 4

When Nazrul Brother pushed me, I returned to reality and told him everything. Even the courier person like him was pretty shocked by my words. He immediately said to me,

- But you buried your wife with your own hands, and besides, according to you, she didn't have a twin sister, but how did this girl resemble your wife? And if she has no connection with your wife, how did she know so much about you and your wife?

Hearing so many questions from Nazrul brother, I looked at him like a donkey, but no sound came out of my hearing. I am looking for answers to the questions he asked me.

Nazrul brother breathed a sigh of relief and said,

- Let us come closer to the mystery. The rest will be known tomorrow.

That is why he told everything to the boss in charge of the courier office. He was also shocked to hear these events and immediately said,

- Brother, if you need any help, I will do it. The end of this mystery is making me very interested to know.

Nazrul brother was thrilled to hear such an assurance from the man and said,

-Thank you very much, brother. But you have to help us a little. I know the girl has come here for the last three days to deliver the parcel to you so she will come tomorrow as well. Your job is to call us when she comes here and keep her standing with different words.

Yes, brother, of course.

We both left the courier office and left for home. On the way, Nazrul brother said to me,

-Tomorrow, both of them have to take leave from the office and come to the courier office early in the morning. Because we can't catch the girl if we are too late? But one thing is playing well in my head: she might be your wife's twin sister because someone else can't have such an exact look.

- But neither my mother-in-law nor my wife ever told me anything about her sister.

- Maybe there is a reason behind it. In any case, what is the real story that will be understood tomorrow?

I came home with a lot of excitement. I accidentally left today's parcel at that courier office, but I don't think this parcel will be used after yesterday. Mimi suddenly called me in these thoughts. On her call, I returned from the world of thought to reality and asked,

- What happened?

- No, come to eat.

I followed her to the dining table and saw that my

father-in-law and brother-in-law Mihad were sitting waiting for me to come. Mimi was putting the food on everyone's plates one by one. At one point, Mimi looked at me and said in a slightly hesitant manner,

-Listen! Did you withdraw money from the bank for my father?

I gestured slightly at Mimi's words and said,

- Oops! I didn't remember at all. Today the work in the office was so stressful that I did not remember to go to the bank when I arrived. I will bring it tomorrow.

Mimi remained silent on my words, but looking at her father-in-law, I realized he was pretty angry. I said with a little smile in my mind.

- Will borrow money from me and get angry with me!!

When I finished eating and came to the bedroom, Mimi ran after me.

- Well, try to give money tomorrow. The season of sowing vegetable seeds is passing, so if the father is late, he will not be able to do everything on time.

- Well, I will give it tomorrow.

After successfully comforting Mimi, I prepared for sleep. I fell into a deep sleep, thinking about what would happen tomorrow.

I called Nazrul brother and told him to get up early and said,

-You get ready. I'm leaving in a little while.

In the meantime, both of us have taken leave. Although taking a rest in a government job is challenging, having an intelligent person like Nazrul brother, taking a break is not much of a problem.

Then we arrived at the courier office by bus.

Sitting in a hotel quite far from the courier office, we ordered tea one after another, but the man's call was still not coming. However, Nazrul's brother tried calling the man after 20 minutes to find out if the girl had come, but I was always getting frustrated hearing his unintelligible words. However, the excitement did not seem to sting a bit.

When the man's call came at precisely twelve or fifteen minutes, I excitedly told Nazrul brother,

-Brother, give the loudspeaker.

As he received the call as I said and put it on the loudspeaker, the man from the other side whispered,

-Brother, the girl has arrived! Come a little sooner.

- Well, brother, I'm coming now. You make her stand up somehow.

- Hmm, bro, I'm trying.

After hanging up the phone, we got up from the chair and left the hotel. I somehow handed over a $100 from my pocket to the restaurant's cashier and ran after Nazrul brother. In the meantime, the restaurant's cashier called and said,

- My brother, you would get back $50.

From far away, I said out loud,

- That's your bonus.

Meanwhile, the closer I get to the courier office, my heart rate increases. Why do I feel like I will have a heart attack before I get to the courier office because of all the excitement? Entering the courier office with a lot of curiosity, I saw a girl standing there talking to the guys in charge. I could not see her face till then as she was turned. Before me, Nazrul brother went to the girl and said,

- How are you?

Suddenly hearing such a question from a stranger,

the girl naturally looked at him suspiciously and asked,

-Who are you? I didn't recognize you.

Nazrul brother pointed his finger at me and said,

- Even if you don't know me, you probably know him very well.

When the girl looked at me, the new parcel immediately fell from her hand to the ground. Her entire face was covered with sweat and both his hands began to tremble with an unknown fear. She probably never thought that I would suddenly appear in front of her like this.

I, Nazrul brother, and that girl who is my wife are sitting in a restaurant. Looking at the girl's face, I could tell that she was probably terrified. But I know why I got a feel like Nishi in her face. Suddenly, Nazrul brother said,

- Now tell us everything. Why were you sending him such strange parcels, and what is your relationship with his ex-wife?

The girl mumbled a little and said,

-Actually, Nishi and I were twin sisters. But my father died before we were born, and my mother became very helpless. After the birth of our two sisters, the mother saw that she could not take care of both of them together and adopted Nishi to a childless couple of a large family.

Nazrul brother thought for a while and suddenly said to the girl,

- I understand everything, but I can't match two and two and four in one aspect. How do you know much if you are his first wife's sister? And whether his wife committed suicide or was murdered, he, as a husband, is in confusion.

- Despite the family distance between Nishi and me, I always had a perfect relationship with her, so she used to share everything with me.

No matter how much you share, you are not supposed to know such profound things. And since the divorce paper came a month after his wife's death, it was signed by his wife, so the mystery is turning in the other direction, sister.

I was pretty surprised to hear Nazrul brother's words, but I did not understand anything. On the other hand, I looked at the girl and saw her face was again covered with sweat. Just then, Nazrul brother furrowed his brows and, with a somewhat mysterious smile on his face, said,

- What do you know? His wife was none other than you, and the one who was murdered was your sister. You may have exchanged yourselves that day for some reason, but the divorce papers issued a month later broke all the mystery arrows.

In the words of Nazrul brother, a word came to my heart, what is he saying? Immediately I looked at the girl; she also looked at me for a while. And soon after, she covered her face and started crying. Does that mean she was my Nishi? I then held back the tears in my eyes with great difficulty and asked in a calm voice,

- Why did you do that, Nishi? Did I not love you?

Nishi was still crying. Maybe she did not think that after a long year, she would appear in front of me like this. Nishi's heart was torn for some time, and she said,

- I didn't do all this of my own will, and I didn't even know that day I would lose my sister because of my little love.

Nishi paused for a while and said again,

- You remember the day you went to California for office work? The day before that, I went to my father's house with a strong desire to see my mother. So with much wisdom, I convinced Sumi to leave her at our house for a few days, and I went to stay with my mother. As I shared everything with Sumi, she knew how to behave with my family, so she did not get caught for her behavior. But that afternoon, you told me you would visit California for some time.

I didn't even have time to replace myself with her so quickly. So I explained everything to her over the phone. I don't know how my sister managed everything with you, but I was afraid she would be caught every moment after I sent you. But even if she survived you, she could not save her own life.

This is why Nishi cried. Hearing her words, I could not stop my tears. In this way, after we both hid our pain for a while, Nazrul brother said in a soft tone from the side,

-Actually, this incident has shaken my mind. It seems that this incident will beat any fairy tale. However, inevitably, Sumi did not commit suicide. But who killed her?

Nishi replied,

-The guard would never have the courage to kill Sumi even though he had often looked at me with evil eyes. But I suspect one.

I looked at her with a very cheerful look and asked,

-Who?

- Your uncle. That is, the father of your current wife! Because when he often visited our house, he threatened me with various threats to leave you. Because I was sitting in his daughter's place, he would not tolerate it in any way.

Nishi's words immediately filled my heart with violence and anger. Does he mean that this bad boy's robbery habit has not decreased yet? When I got up from the chair in anger, Nazrul brother took my hand and forced me to sit again.

-Brother! If you do something now in anger, he will probably escape. We need to collect the evidence and act with cold intelligence.

I calmed down a bit by his words and asked,

- Where can I get proof?

- Inside the prison! It means that the security guard who was implicated in a false case knows the events of that day at least a little. Now our task is to visit him in jail.

At Nazrul brother's words, I said,

- He is in Central Prison Now.

- Let's talk to his family to know his prisoner number.

After that, we went to the central prison to talk to that security guard after crossing many ups and downs. Meanwhile, my wife Mimi keeps calling. On receiving the call, she said from the other side,

- Did you withdraw the money from the bank? Probably you will forget again, that's why I reminded you again.

Although I had much anger in my heart, I kept it in my mind and said in a calm voice,

- Yes, I am coming with money.

Mimi was pleased with my words and said,

- Well, be careful.

I hung up the call and said to myself,

- You will know whether I am bringing money or not after a few moments.

On seeing me, the security guard ran from the other side of the prison and hugged my legs, and said,

-Brother, believe that I have not done anything terrible to Nishi madam even in my life, and I have not even hit her. I have been framed in a false case, and my wife and children have been made orphans.

Seeing the porter's cry, my heart softened a little, but immediately I said to him in a firm voice,

- If you don't kill, who is killing Nishi?

- Brother, I honestly do not know. By Allah

Hearing his words, Nazrul brother said,

-Well, you think one thing! Did anyone look for Maruf brother after he went to California for office work?

The security guard thought for a while and replied,

- Yes, brother. One man came.

I said curiously.

- Who came?

- A half-grown man! He had come to your house before. It seems that was your uncle!

Nazrul brother jumped up and said,

-Yes! Two and two and four are matched. Well, don't worry. You will be out of jail in two days if you are innocent.

Hearing Nazrul brother's words, the security guard's eyes sparkled with happiness.

I already understood then that Nishi's murderer was none other than my uncle in a relationship with my current father-in-law. In the meantime, I, Nazrul brother, and Nishi appeared in front of our house with the police. It's half past midnight.

Although Mimi called me many times due to my

lateness, I did not receive it. Because I want to appear before him like lightning. When the police wanted to enter inside, Nazrul brother stopped them and said,

- Wait, let's make the proof a little stronger. Maruf brother, please give me your father-in-law's number.

As he said, I gave him the number of Mimi's father. He put it on the dial list and called. Nazrul brother turned on the loudspeaker as soon as he received the call. From the other side, my father-in-law said,

- Hello, who is saying?

- I'm telling you. What do you remember? A year ago, you killed a girl and hanged an innocent security guard only to marry your daughter to a boy named Maruf?

My father-in-law stammered a little.

-Who are you? And what are you talking about at night?

-I have all the evidence of the girl you killed and proof that you have bribed the police to reverse the post-mortem report.

Now my father-in-law was very scared and said,

- Brother, who are you?

- Even if you don't know who I am, it is not a matter. But if you don't reveal these to me, I won't do it. But if you don't come to my message address within an hour, do you know what will happen?

-Brother, brother...

Before the father-in-law could say anything, Nazrul Brother hung up the phone. Then he wrote something in the message and looked at us with a mysterious smile, and said,

- Brother, the work is done, and we rather wait here.

As he said, we were standing in front of the gate for five minutes, and we heard the sound of someone rushing down the stairs. Seeing us standing with the police in front of the entrance, my father-in-law was startled like a ghost. But the most surprised to see Nishi. Because he thinks he killed Nishi, then how did she come here?

When the two police officers caught him, he tried unsuccessfully to free himself and said,

- Why are you catching me? What have I done?

Nazrul brother went to him and said,

- Ah, the older man does not know what he is doing. Behold, I am raising her whom you killed from her grave. She told us how she was beaten. Don't you see that the shirt is worn upside down while going to the message address?

The word of this wretched father-in-law, whom a dacoit touched, slowly spread everywhere, including in my house. Mimi faints again and again because of her father's bad behavior. Where my mother stood up to get Mimi married to me, today she spat on her sister and Mimi on sight.

I am sitting with Nishi on a park bench. No words are coming out of anyone's mouth. I broke the silence and said to Nishi,

- You survived that day. Why didn't you come to me that day?

- I still don't know why I didn't come that day, but I was terrified. Moreover, my mother was fighting with death, and if she had heard that the girl she had brought up so much had been killed, she would not have survived. And since your aunt has done so much to get her daughter married to you, I didn't want to stand in her way anymore. Still, the fire of revenge was burning in my heart, so I wanted to punish him through you from behind.

- Well then, can't we start life again as before?

- No, because I divorced you long ago.

- But I didn't sign it.

- Even if you don't sign, it will be done after three months. And your wife is not at fault here; she didn't know anything about this.

In a moment, Nishi turned away from me and said,

-Besides, I am happy with the new one. I hope you stay satisfied with your wife.

With this, Nishi walked on the small grass of the park towards the unknown. I know very well that Nishi is crying because no one can soothe the pain in her heart at the moment of leaving.

After saying goodbye to Nishi and coming home, I saw both Mimi and Mihad preparing to leave the house along with my mother-in-law. But no one present in the place is stopping them. Instead, everyone has an apparent hatred towards them. Seeing me, Mimi bowed her head and slowly left the room with the other two.

As soon as they left, Nazrul brother pushed me from behind and said,

-Damn, the brother, are you stupid? Nishi is lost. Now, will they lose this too? They have no fault here.

As he said, the moment I suddenly left the room, he asked,

- Where do you go?

- Brother, I have already done two marriages, so I don't want to marry again. So I am going to bring my wife.

Hearing my words, Nazrul brother said with a

devilish smile,

- When will you give the reward for the fact that I did so much spying for you?

- Bring the wife first, and then I will give you everything you need.

That's why I ran out of the house. Because no matter what, I will never have a wife like Mimi, and I want her anyway

ABOUT THE AUTHOR

IQ MISKAL is an author of mystery for **ENVELOPE, MYSTERY OF ERROR & SHINY CAT**. He was born in an Asian country and most of his time spend in Asian country. When not writing, he can be found in his office, talking the people with knowledgeable topic.

www.ingramcontent.com/pod-product-compliance
Lightning Source LLC
LaVergne TN
LVHW020527160826
845677LV00015B/3939

* 9 7 9 8 3 5 4 3 8 0 1 0 7 *